First edition for the United States, its Dependencies, Canada, and the Philippines published in 2008 by Barron's Educational Series, Inc.
© Copyright 2008 by *b small publishing*, Surrey, UK.

All inquiries should be addressed to:
Barron's Educational Series, Inc.
250 Wireless Boulevard
Hauppauge, NY 11788
www.barronseduc.com

ISBN-13: 978-0-7641-4047-1
ISBN-10: 0-7641-4047-7

Library of Congress Control Number: 2008925396

Printed in China
9 8 7 6 5 4 3 2 1

Danny's Blog

El blog de Daniel

Stephen Rabley

Pictures by Martin Ursell
Spanish by Rosa María Martín

Daniel Molinero vive en Borneo.

Su madre es la directora de la reserva
de orangutanes en Pumai.

Pumai es un lugar muy bonito, con muchos árboles.

A Daniel le encanta, y le encantan los orangutanes.

Su favorito se llama Gloria. Tiene sólo dos años.

No tiene padre ni madre. Daniel la cuida.

Cada mañana, antes de la escuela, le da leche
y un plátano.

Danny Miller lives in Borneo.
His Mom is the director of the orangutan reserve
at Pumai. Pumai is a very beautiful place with lots of
trees. Danny loves it, and he loves the orangutans.
His favorite is called Gloria. She's only two years old.
She has no mother or father. Danny looks after her.
Every morning, before school, he gives her some milk
and a banana.

Hoy es sábado. Daniel ayuda a su amigo Pablo.

Pablo es guía. Trabaja para la reserva.

"Hay muy pocos orangutanes salvajes en el mundo",
Pablo explica a los turistas.

"¿Qué significa la palabra *orangután*?" pregunta el hombre.

"Significa hombre de la selva", dice Pablo.

"¿Son peligrosos?" pregunta la niña.

"No", dice Daniel. "Son muy tímidos.
Y son inteligentes también."

Son muy tímidos.
They are very shy.

¿Son peligrosos?
Are they dangerous?

Today is Saturday. Danny is helping his friend, Paul.
Paul is a guide. He works at the reserve.
"There are very few wild *orangutans* in the world,"
Paul explains to the tourists.
"What does the word *orangutan* mean?" asks the man.
"It means man of the forest," says Paul.
"Are they dangerous?" asks the young girl.
"No," says Danny. "They are very shy.
And they're clever, too."

La tarde siguiente, Daniel está viendo las noticias en televisión.

De repente, su madre entra en el cuarto.

"¿Puedo hablar contigo?" pregunta. Parece preocupada.

Daniel apaga el televisor. "¿Qué pasa, mamá?"

"Necesitamos 50.000 dólares para la reserva antes del mes próximo. No los tengo." Mira un papel que tiene en la mano. "Pero tengo esto."

The next evening, Danny is watching the news on TV. Suddenly, his Mom comes into the room. "Can I talk to you?" she asks. She looks worried. Danny turns off the TV. "What's wrong, Mom?" "We need 50,000 dollars for the reserve before next month. I don't have it." She looks at the piece of paper in her hand. "But I have this."

Daniel toma el papel. Es un correo electrónico.
"Querida señora Molinero", lee. "Mi nombre es Brad
Coram y soy el jefe de la compañía maderera Borneo.
Quiero comprar su reserva…"
"Es muy sencillo", dice la mamá de Daniel. "Brad Coram
quiere cortar nuestros árboles. Él es rico y nosotros no.
Lo siento, Daniel, pero esto es el fin de Pumai."
Por la noche, Daniel no puede dormir.
Piensa en la compañía maderera Borneo.

Danny takes the piece of paper. It's an e-mail.

"Dear Mrs. Miller," he reads. "My name is Brad Coram and I'm the boss of the Borneo Wood Company. I want to buy your reserve…"

"It's very simple," says Danny's Mom. "Brad Coram wants to cut down our trees. He's rich and we're not. I'm sorry, Danny, but this is the end for Pumai."

At night, Danny can't sleep.

He is thinking about the Borneo Wood Company.

La mañana siguiente Daniel está con Gloria, como siempre.

"¿Qué vamos a hacer?" susurra.

Camino de la escuela, Daniel está muy triste.

No habla con sus amigos en el autobús.

Mira fijamente por la ventana.

"No está bien", piensa. "Mamá no puede vender la reserva.

Los orangutanes la necesitan. Necesitan la selva.

¡Tiene que haber otra solución!"

Next morning, Danny is with Gloria, as usual.

"What are we going to do?" he whispers.

On the way to school, Danny is very sad.

He doesn't talk to his friends on the bus.

He stares out of the window.

"This isn't right," he thinks. "Mom can't sell the reserve.

The orangutans need it. They need the forest.

There must be another answer!"

15

En la escuela, Daniel tiene una clase de informática.
La profesora escribe 'BLOG' en la pizarra.
"¿Qué significa esta palabra?" pregunta.
Daniel no contesta. Está pensando en los problemas
de la reserva.
"Es un diario de Internet", dice un niño."Mucha gente
los escribe. Puedes leer cosas sobre sus vidas."
De repente, Daniel sonríe.
"*Sí*", dice. "¡Ésa es la solución!"

12

At school, Danny has a computer class.
The teacher writes 'BLOG' on the board.
"What does this word mean?" she asks.
Danny doesn't answer. He's still thinking about
the reserve's problems.
"It's an Internet diary," one boy says. "Lots of people
write them. You can read about their lives."
Suddenly, Danny smiles.
"*Yes*," he says. "That's the answer!"

Esa tarde Daniel habla con su madre.

"Tengo una idea", dice. "Primero, voy a empezar un blog

Voy a hablarle a la gente de la reserva de Pumai y de la

compañía maderera Borneo. Entonces pueden enviar corre

a Brad Coram diciendo: *No compre la reserva de Pumai*."

"Bien", dice ella muy despacio. "Pero, ¿y el dinero?

Necesitamos 50.000 dólares."

Daniel sonríe. "Ésa es mi segunda idea."

Daniel se la dice mientras lavan los platos.

14

That evening, Danny talks to his Mom.
"I've got an idea," he says. "First, I'm going to start a blog.
I'm going to tell people about the reserve at Pumai and
the Borneo Wood Company. Then they can send e-mails
to Brad Coram and say: *Don't buy Pumai's reserve.*"
"OK," she says very slowly. "But what about the money?
We still need 50,000 dollars."
Danny smiles. "That's my second idea."
Danny tells her all about it, while they wash the dishes.

Después de cenar, Daniel abre su computadora portátil.
Primero escribe sobre Pumai y los orangutanes.
Después escribe sobre la compañía maderera Borneo.
Al final dice: "Por favor envíen este mensaje a Brad Coram: *La
reserva de Pumai es importante. No la compre y no corte los árboles.*
Gloria está comiendo una naranja. Daniel la mira y sonríe.
"¡A ver qué pasa ahora, Gloria!"

After dinner, Danny opens his laptop.

First, he writes about Pumai and the orangutans.

Next, he writes about the Borneo Wood Company.

Finally, he says, "Please send this message to Brad Coram: *The reserve at Pumai is important. Don't buy it and cut down the trees.*"

Gloria is eating an orange. Danny looks at her and smiles. "Let's see what happens now, Gloria!"

Cuatro días después, Brad Coram vuelve de un viaje de
negocios. Encuentra cientos de correos sobre Pumai.
Vienen de África, Australia, Sudamérica, Norteamérica,
Europa, Asia… ¡de todo el mundo!
Mucha gente está enfadada con su compañía.
Pero no hay ningún correo de la señora Molinero.
Llama a Pumai, y la mamá de Daniel contesta.
"¡Pare el blog de su hijo, señora Molinero!" dice.
"¡Oh! ¿Hay un problema?" dice la mamá de Daniel.

18

Four days later, Brad Coram returns from a business trip.
He finds hundreds of e-mails about Pumai.
They're from Africa, Australia, South America, North
America, Europe, Asia… all over the world!
A lot of people are angry with his company.
But there is no e-mail from Mrs. Miller.
He calls Pumai, and Danny's Mom answers.
"Stop your son's blog, Mrs. Miller!" he says.
"Oh! Is there a problem?" says Danny's Mom.

Entonces recuerda la segunda idea de Daniel.
"Bien, venga mañana a las seis con 50.000
dólares", dice. "Podemos hablar entonces."
Brad Coram está contento. "Necesita dinero", piensa.
"En unas semanas todos olvidarán ese estúpido
blog, y puedo comprar la reserva."
"Bien. Hasta mañana, señora Molinero", dice.
La madre de Daniel sonríe. Llama a otro número.
"Aló, ¿Telenoticias Borneo?"

Then she remembers Danny's second idea.

"OK, come here tomorrow at six o'clock with 50,000 dollars," she says. "We can talk about it then."

Brad Coram is pleased. "She needs money," he thinks. "In a few weeks everyone's going to forget this stupid blog. Then I can buy Pumai's reserve."

"Fine. See you tomorrow, Mrs. Miller," he says.

Danny's Mom smiles. She calls another number.

"Hello. Is this Borneo TV News?"

Al día siguiente Brad Coram va en coche a Pumai.

La mamá de Daniel está esperándolo.

"Hola, señora Molinero", dice Brad. "Tengo el dinero.
¿Dónde podemos hablar?"

La mamá de Daniel lo lleva a su oficina.

En la puerta le dice: "¿Puede sostener a Gloria
un momento, por favor?"

Le da el bebé orangután a Brad Coram.

"Pase, por favor", dice, abriendo la puerta.

Next day, Brad Coram drives to Pumai.

Danny's Mom is waiting for him.

"Hello, Mrs. Miller," says Brad. "I've got the money.

Where can we talk?"

Danny's Mom takes him to her office.

At the door she says, "Can you hold Gloria

for a minute, please?"

She gives the baby orangutan to Brad Coram.

"Please, after you," she says, as she opens the door.

Brad Coram entra en la oficina.

Ve una cámara de televisión y a tres personas.

Una mujer le sonríe.

"Buenas tardes, Sr. Coram. Me llamo Corina Pek y soy de Telenoticias Borneo", dice.

"Quiero hacerle unas preguntas."

"¿Está grabando?" pregunta Brad Coram.

"Sí, está usted hablando en directo para las noticias de las seis."

Brad Coram walks into the office.

He sees a TV camera and three people.

A woman smiles at him.

"Good evening, Mr. Coram. My name is Corina Pek, and I'm from Borneo TV," she says. "I have some questions for you."

"Are you filming?" asks Brad Coram.

"Yes. You're on the six o'clock news right now."

Brad Coram mira la cámara de televisión.

"¿Qué opina de la reserva, señor Coram?"
pregunta Corina.

"Es muy… bonita", dice Brad.

"¿Y es importante la labor que se realiza en Pumai?"

"Sí, sí, claro."

"¿Y por qué está usted aquí hoy? ¿Quiere comprar la
reserva y cortar los árboles? Al fin y al cabo, usted
es el jefe de la compañía maderera Borneo."

Brad Coram looks at the TV camera.
"What do you think of the reserve, Mr. Coram?"
asks Corina.
"It's very… beautiful," says Brad.
"And the work being done at Pumai, is it important?"
"Yes, yes, of course."
"And why are you here today? Do you want to
buy Pumai and cut down its trees? After all, you
are the boss of Borneo Wood."

¿Por qué está usted
aquí hoy?

Why are you here
today?

27

Brad Coram mira a la cámara. Traga saliva.

"No, claro que no", dice. "Quiero... *dar* a la reserva 50.000 dólares." Saca el cheque de su bolsillo.

"Aquí tiene."

"*¿De verdad?* Muchas gracias", dice la mamá de Daniel. "Podemos hacer muchas cosas con este dinero."

Fuera, Brad Coram ve a Daniel y a Pablo.

Brad mira a Daniel. Daniel mira a Brad. No hablan.

Brad va directamente a su coche.

Brad Coram looks at the camera. He swallows hard.
"No, of course not," he says. "I want to… *give* the reserve
50,000 dollars." He takes a check out of his pocket.
"Here it is."
"*Really?* Thank you very much," says Danny's Mom.
"We can do a lot with this money."
Outside, Brad Coram sees Danny and Paul.
He looks at Danny. Danny looks at Brad. They don't speak.
Brad walks straight to his car.

Cinco días después, Pablo tiene un montón de cheques.
"¡Esto es fantástico!" dice. "Cientos de personas están
enviando dinero para ayudar a nuestra reserva y a los
orangutanes."

La mamá de Daniel sonríe. "Hay muchos correos también
Mira, éste lo dice todo."

Les enseña la computadora y todos ríen.

Las palabras de la pantalla dicen:

¡Viva el blog de Daniel!

Five days later, Paul has a big pile of checks.

"This is fantastic!" he says. "Hundreds of people are
sending money to help our reserve and the orangutans."

Danny's Mom smiles. "There are many e-mails, too.
Look, this one says it all."

She shows them her computer and they laugh.

The words on the screen say:

Hurray for Danny's blog!

Quiz

You will need some paper and a pencil.

1 Here are three things that Gloria likes. Copy the pictures and write the Spanish words. They are on story pages 2 and 16.

2 Two of these sentences are false. Can you change them to make them true? Then say them.

Pablo trabaja para la reserva en Pumai.

Los orangutanes son peligrosos.

Danny escribe un blog.

Los orangutanes necesitan la selva.

Brad Coram no es rico.

3 Copy this e-mail message and fill in the gaps. Choose one sentence from question 2 to complete your email.

Me llamo [your name] y soy de [your town].

La labor que se hace en Pumai es importante.

No corte los árboles! _____